ANIMAL ENGINEERS

Honeybees

by Rebecca Pettiford

BLASTOFF! READERS 3

BELLWETHER MEDIA • MINNEAPOLIS, MN

Blastoff! Readers are carefully developed by literacy experts to build reading stamina and move students toward fluency by combining standards-based content with developmentally appropriate text.

Level 1 provides the most support through repetition of high-frequency words, light text, predictable sentence patterns, and strong visual support.

Level 2 offers early readers a bit more challenge through varied sentences, increased text load, and text-supportive special features.

Level 3 advances early-fluent readers toward fluency through increased text load, less reliance on photos, advancing concepts, longer sentences, and more complex special features.

★ **Blastoff! Universe**

This edition first published in 2025 by Bellwether Media, Inc.

Library of Congress Cataloging-in-Publication Data

LC record for Honeybees available at: https://lccn.loc.gov/2024015046

Editor: Rachael Barnes Designer: Josh Brink

Printed in the United States of America, North Mankato, MN.

Table of Contents

Nest Builders

Honeybees are flying **insects**. They make honey. Honeybees live in **colonies** that include workers, **drones**, and a queen.

Colonies live in nests made of honeycomb. Nests keep bees and their food safe.

colony

Honeybees first came from Europe. Today, they can be found around the world. There are several honeybee **species**.

Honeybee Range Map

Honeybees live in flowering areas like gardens and **meadows**.

Planning a Nest

New colonies often begin in the spring. The new queen is growing. The old queen and many workers leave their nest. They fly away in a **swarm**.

Workers scout for the best site to build a new nest.

Workers look for places with food and water. They often choose hollow trees, fences, or buildings.

worker drinking water

Workers do a waggle dance
when they find a site!
This tells the colony to fly
to their new home.

Time to Build!

Workers make honey from **nectar**. Then they turn honey into sugar inside their bodies.

The sugar becomes liquid wax. It leaves workers' bodies through their **wax glands**. The wax quickly hardens.

Building Materials

Workers rub the hard wax off their bodies using their hairy back legs.

They pass the wax to their middle legs and then to their **mandibles**. They chew it to make it soft again.

Workers use the wax to build thousands of six-sided cells. This forms the honeycomb. It can take one to eight weeks to complete.

Honeycombs store eggs, young bees, and honey. Adult bees rest in the cells.

young bees

cell

The Nest Is Ready!

The nest is done! Next, older workers make **propolis**. This mix of **saliva**, wax, and **resin** has many uses.

Propolis covers holes and cracks in the honeycomb. Honeybees also use it as medicine!

Some colonies are hurt by **colony collapse disorder**. Beekeepers build homes called hives to help keep colonies together.

Honeybees continue to build nests. They are safe and strong. The honeycomb can last for centuries!

Inside a Honeybee Nest

- honeycomb is made of beeswax and has thousands of cells
- cells house the queen, eggs, honey, and other bees

Glossary

colonies—groups of honeybees; colonies live together in the same nest.

colony collapse disorder—a condition that causes nearly all of the adult worker bees to leave their colony and disappear

drones—male bees that mate with queen bees

insects—small animals with six legs and hard outer bodies; an insect's body is divided into three parts.

mandibles—one of the two parts of the mouth on some insects; mandibles are often used for biting, chewing, cutting, and digging.

meadows—fields of grass

nectar—a sweet liquid made by plants

propolis—a mixture made of honeybee saliva, wax, and resin

resin—a substance that dries clear and is often used to keep surfaces safe from harm

saliva—a watery liquid made in the mouth

species—kinds of animals

swarm—a large group of bees gathered together in one place

wax glands—body parts on worker honeybees that make beeswax

To Learn More

AT THE LIBRARY

Holasová, Aneta Františka. *Bruno the Beekeeper: A Honey Primer.* Somerville, Mass.: Candlewick Press, 2021.

Nargi, Lela. *The Book of Bees: Inside the Hives and Lives of Honeybees, Bumblebees, Cuckoo Bees, and Other Busy Buzzers.* New York, N.Y.: Black Dog & Leventhal Publishers, 2022.

Pettiford, Rebecca. *Ants.* Minneapolis, Minn.: Bellwether Media, 2025.

ON THE WEB

FACTSURFER

Factsurfer.com gives you a safe, fun way to find more information.

1. Go to www.factsurfer.com.

2. Enter "honeybees" into the search box and click 🔍.

3. Select your book cover to see a list of related content.

Index

The images in this book are reproduced through the courtesy of: mykhailo pavlenko, cover (hero); 46design, back cover; Alexander Wallstrom, p. 3; Terry Kelly, p. 4; M Vilaret, pp. 4-5; Daniel Prudek, pp. 6-7, 15 (honeybee); MakroBetz, pp. 8-9; Donna Bollenbach, p. 9; UrbanRadim, pp. 10-11; Thanapong Hundee, p. 11; Goodly Pixels, pp. 12-13; MakeStory Studio, p. 13 (honey); StudioSmart, p. 13 (wax); Daisy-Daisy/ iStock, pp. 14-15; gerard lacz/ Alamy, 15 (wax glands); khlungcenter, p. 15 (mandibles), slowmotiongli, p. 16 (young bees); Nikolay Petkov, pp. 16-17; kosolovskyy, pp. 18-19; Vera Larina, pp. ˉ9, 21 (cells); Maarten Zeehandelaar, p. 20; VECTOR SPACE, pp. 20-21 (honeybee nest); Dionisvera, p. 21 (honey); Samo Trebizan, p. 21 (queen); Ihor Hvozdetskyi, p. 21 (eggs); Shaiith, p. 23.